Fairy Felicity's Moonlight Adventure

nosy crow

Alison Murray

One warm summer night, at the end of the day,
the fairies were waking up, ready to play.
When Fairy Felicity opened her door,
she spotted a letter, right there on the floor.
A message said, 'Follow the silvery snail.
You'll find a surprise at the end of the trail!'

"I'm here!" called the snail.

"Follow me. Quick, let's go!"

"Oh, gosh," said the fairy.

"I thought snails were slow!"

She followed the
snail trail wherever it led.
"But where is it going?"
Felicity said.

A moth joined in too, and they flew through the night,
tracking the trail that was sparkly and bright.

They went through the greenhouse and over the pots . . .

. . . and met a bright ladybird covered in spots.

Then down in the orchard
they wound round the trees,
and on past the hives that
were buzzing with bees.

"Dear Dragonfly, join us," Felicity said . . .

. . . as Moth, Bee and Ladybird raced on ahead.

They wove through the foxgloves,
and circled the roses,
and hopped over daisies that
tickled their noses.

At the end of the garden
they came to a wall,
where the ivy was thick and
the grass was so tall.

And there, by an old door,
the snail stopped and said,
"This way, Miss Felicity
— just mind your head."

She crept through the gap
where the dandelions grew . . .

"Surprise!"
cried her friends.

"Happy Birthday to you!"

For Carole
A.M.

First published in 2016 by Nosy Crow Ltd

The Crow's Nest, 10a Lant Street

London SE1 1QR

www.nosycrow.com

ISBN 978 0 85763 581 5 (HB)

ISBN 978 0 85763 588 4 (PB)

A CIP catalogue record for this book is available

from the British Library.

Printed in China by Imago

Papers used by Nosy Crow are made from wood grown in sustainable forests.

1 3 5 7 9 8 6 4 2 (HB)

1 3 5 7 9 8 6 4 2 (PB)